SONY PICTURES
ANIMATION

ViVo™

Movie Novelization

Adapted by Ximena Hastings

Simon Spotlight
New York London T

This book is a work of fiction. Any references to historical events, real people, or real places are used fictitiously. Other names, characters, places, and events are products of the author's imagination, and any resemblance to actual events or places or persons, living or dead, is entirely coincidental.

SONY PICTURES ANIMATION

SIMON SPOTLIGHT

An imprint of Simon & Schuster Children's Publishing Division

1230 Avenue of the Americas, New York, New York 10020

This Simon Spotlight edition July 2021

Copyright © 2021 Sony Pictures Animation. All Rights Reserved. All rights reserved, including the right of reproduction in whole or in part in any form. SIMON SPOTLIGHT and colophon are registered trademarks of Simon & Schuster, Inc. For information about special discounts for bulk purchases, please contact Simon & Schuster Special Sales at 1-866-506-1949 or business@simonandschuster.com.

Book designed by Nicholas Sciacca

The text of this book was set in Archer Medium.

Manufactured in the United States of America 0621 OFF

10 9 8 7 6 5 4 3 2 1

ISBN 978-1-5344-6581-7 (pbk)

ISBN 978-1-5344-6582-4 (eBook)

Chapter One
One of a Kind

It was a beautiful day in Havana, Cuba. The ocean waves danced lightly on the shore, while the people of the city started waking. Locals began opening up their shops as tourists strolled the colorful streets.

In the Plaza Vieja, an old man named Andrés started setting up his music

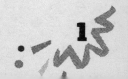

stand with his kinkajou, Vivo. They had been playing music together ever since Vivo arrived in Havana several years ago. The two of them had grown to become best friends and musical partners.

Andrés grabbed his harmonica and then turned to Vivo.

"Are you ready?" Andrés asked Vivo.

Vivo nodded, and then the two of them began to perform.

As soon as they started playing, the streets of Havana came to life. Andrés and Vivo played maracas, drums, a guitar—they played it all! Vivo even joined Andrés in singing! As they continued to play, more and more people started

gathering around the plaza. Andrés and Vivo had played music together so long, Vivo could even finish Andrés's musical phrases. They didn't have to understand each other's language, because *music* was their language!

"*Eso,* Vivo!" Andrés cheered, as Vivo danced and hit the drums. The crowd began to clap as well, joining in the fun. This was the best part of Vivo's day. He couldn't imagine a life without music, or a life without Andrés.

"Bravo!" cried the audience when Andrés and Vivo finished playing.

"Good show, Vivo!" Andrés said.

Vivo chirped in agreement.

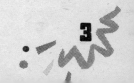

Andrés put his arm around Vivo's back and then the two of them sat to look at the audience. Andrés peeled a mango for Vivo, and the two of them ate peacefully side-by-side, enjoying the bustle of the plaza. People came and went, most of them accustomed to seeing the old man and his kinkajou together, some of them stopping by to take pictures or ask about their instruments.

Vivo loved watching Andrés describe his instruments or play small tunes for kids. Andrés was the reason Vivo fell in love with music, after all. Andrés's passion and true love of music was so inspiring to Vivo. Andrés was the best

4

teacher, and there was no one else like him.

The duo finished up their snack and then went off to the Malecón wall, where they'd have their next performance of the day.

Vivo grinned. He couldn't wait to see what the rest of the day had in store!

Chapter Two
The Letter

While Andrés and Vivo were preparing for their next performance, a man suddenly ran up to them. *"Oiga!* Andrés! You have a letter!" the man, named Montoya, said. Montoya was Andrés and Vivo's neighbor. He was a friendly man with a warm smile, who had a kind heart and a fierce spirit. He ran over to

them and passed the letter along.

"*Gracias, amigo,*" Andrés said, thanking him before opening the letter.

As soon as he opened it, Andrés suddenly turned pale. He held his hand up to his chest and then sat against the wall.

"*Marta?* But how can this be?" Andrés asked, in shock.

Who is Marta? Vivo wondered to himself.

Vivo hopped over to Andrés and tried to take a peek at the letter, but had no luck. Overhead, Vivo heard seagulls crying out and wondered if they felt how Andrés looked.

Andrés began to read the letter aloud.

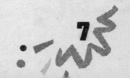

Mi amor, Andrés . . .

What words can I write in a letter after being separated for so many years? As I prepare for retirement, I have been flooded with memories of the beautiful music we made together. I don't know if you can forgive my silence, but nothing would mean more to me than for us to sing together again. My farewell concert is next week at the Mambo Cabana in Miami on June 16th at 9:00. If you are there with your tres, I'll know you feel the same. I hope it's not too late.

Amor, Marta

Andrés looked up from reading, his eyes wide with surprise. But he was not as surprised as Vivo was. He had no idea Andrés used to play music with anyone else!

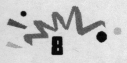

"I can't believe this. Marta Sandoval . . . writing to me after all these years," Andrés said slowly.

"Did you say Marta Sandoval?" a passerby asked.

Soon, other people start crowding around and word quickly spread about Marta's final show. Everyone was talking excitedly. Marta Sandoval was one of the most famous singers, and she rarely performed! The fact that this would be her last show sent everyone in a dizzying panic.

"You have to go," Mrs. Flores, the shopkeeper below Andrés's apartment, urged.

Other people nodded in agreement.

"You can perform together one last time!" another person agreed.

"I'm too old. I can't go to Miami," Andrés said in resignation.

"Of course, you can, *amigo,*" Montoya replied. "We'll all chip in. We're going to send you to Miami!"

The crowd gathered around Andrés and Vivo started to clap and cheer. Then they started to chip in whatever money they could.

Andrés shook his head, but slowly, he seemed to be warming up to the idea. *Imagine a trip to the Mambo Cabana to see Marta after all these years,* Andrés

thought. *I never dreamed this day would happen.*

No one noticed as Vivo jumped and shrieked behind Andrés, still trying to figure out who Marta was and why Andrés had to leave in order to see her.

Chapter Three
Marta

Later that afternoon, Andrés was too shaken to speak. It wasn't until that evening that Andrés pulled out a dusty old box from his closet. He blew the dust away and set it down carefully on the floor. The box was covered in small stickers with different venue names on them. Vivo had never seen it before, but

clearly, this box had a lot of history.

"Marta," Andrés whispered, tracing the letter *M* on the box.

Then Andrés took a deep breath and opened it. Dust flew everywhere, but inside, the items looked pristine. There were dozens of record albums with Andrés's face on them, and there was someone else's face on the albums too . . . Marta. There was a poster announcing their first concert at the Tropicana. Vivo had never seen Andrés smile so widely in any picture or in real life! There were what seemed like hundreds of newspaper clippings with their pictures, and glowing reviews

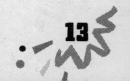

13

about the great duo of Andrés and Marta. But mostly there were pictures of the two of them together. Andrés looked so happy in all of them, and he also looked very much in love.

Vivo picked up one of the album covers.

Andrés smiled sadly. "Marta was the toast of Havana. No one in Cuba could sing like she did. Everyone fell head over heels in love with her ... including me. But I never told her how I felt," Andrés said, looking at the album cover with Vivo. "I wanted to keep things professional. I was just the musician playing piano, after all. She was always the real star."

Andrés picked up another picture and

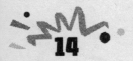

then gazed off into the distance, remembering a memory of the two of them together.

"One night, I decided my moment had come. I had finally gathered up the courage to tell Marta I loved her. But then a promoter from the United States interrupted us, offering Marta a chance of a lifetime—to perform at the Mambo Cabana in Miami. It was her dream come true," Andrés said, sighing sadly. "I knew I would be stopping her if I told her how I felt. So, I let her go. I let her go, Vivo."

Andrés placed the picture against his chest and hung his head. Then he walked

over to his balcony and looked out over Havana. The city was still buzzing at that time of night. It had a soft glow, and there was music in the air. Inside the apartment, though, it was cold and dark. It felt empty.

Andrés turned back inside and pulled out his tres, his three-stringed guitar. He began playing a song.

Vivo watched Andrés intently, still mesmerized by all the items in the box. One by one, he picked them up, wondering how much of his friend's life he had missed. How much he hadn't asked about. Vivo had so many questions, but he knew he had to give his friend some

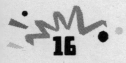

space. He listened as Andrés continued to play the song. Vivo was amazed at how very musically talented his best friend was.

When Andrés had finished playing the song, he looked over at Vivo.

"When Marta left, my love grew. I didn't know any other way to express it, so I wrote her a song. She would never hear this song and it's been too painful to play. Until now," Andrés said.

Andrés looked at the handwritten song longingly. On the top of the envelope it read, *Para mi amor, Marta.*

For my love? Vivo thought. *Wow. This Marta must have been pretty special!*

Suddenly, Andrés's mood changed. He leapt up on his feet and clapped his hands together, determined.

"This is it, Vivo. We have a second chance!" Andrés exclaimed.

"Second what now?" Vivo chirped.

Andrés didn't understand Vivo's noises and sounds, but he continued anyway.

"We are going to the Mambo Cabana! We are going to play this song for Marta so she will finally know that I love her. It's the only way!" Andrés said, pulling out his suitcase.

"Oh … wow … you're serious!" Vivo said.

"I know you're excited, too, *chiquito*," Andrés said, smiling.

"No! You've got me all wrong! I'm not excited!" Vivo said loudly. Andrés looked at him, confused. *"We're plaza musicians. Just two small-town guys. We can't play in Miami!"*

Vivo was so upset he had to leave the room. He climbed out on the balcony and reached for the drain pipe to climb up to the roof. He often went there when he wanted to be alone.

Vivo continued grumbling to himself. He could tell Marta was important to Andrés, but he just couldn't understand why they had to leave their home to see her.

What is he thinking?! Vivo said to himself. *We can't just go all the way to*

Miami! It's been, like, sixty years! What difference will one little song make now?

Vivo looked down at the plaza where he and Andrés met. It was empty now, but the memories came flooding back to Vivo.

There was the time Vivo climbed down a tree to hear Andrés play music, the time Andrés gave Vivo his first instrument and Vivo somehow knew exactly what to do. And then there was the first time they played together. It was like magic. Vivo knew then that even though he was not from Havana, this was his home. And Andrés had agreed. He had taken Vivo in as his own and cared for him. He always looked out for him....

Vivo sighed heavily. He couldn't understand why Andrés would want to give all that up to go to Miami, but he knew he had to look out for his friend's best interests, too. He had to support him, even if that meant going to Miami.

Vivo climbed back down off the roof and went into the apartment, where Andrés was sitting in his armchair, sleeping. Vivo walked over quietly and removed his glasses before placing a warm blanket on his friend.

In the corner, the suitcase lay open and empty.

Well, that suitcase isn't going to pack

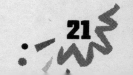

itself, Vivo thought. He walked over to the closet and started to pack for their journey. If his best friend wanted to go to Miami to fulfill his dreams, then that's what the two of them would do.

Chapter Four
Adiós

The next morning, Vivo awoke to a bright ray of sunlight that warmed his belly. He rubbed his eyes and stretched his legs. He was ready to help his friend get to Marta! Vivo hopped down off his bed and opened the balcony doors, shining more light into the room. Already, the plaza outside was bustling with noise and music.

 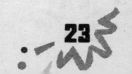

I'll miss Havana, Vivo thought. *But today is the day! And it's a beautiful day to travel!*

Vivo walked over to Andrés, who still looked like he was sleeping. Andrés had fallen asleep holding the song he played the night before.

"Good morning, amigo! Look, I'm sorry about last night, but you shouldn't be sleeping anymore. We have to get going!" Vivo said.

But Andrés didn't move.

Vivo tugged on Andrés's pant leg, but Andrés still didn't wake up.

Suddenly, Vivo froze. There was a strange look on Andrés's face. He

looked peaceful, but too peaceful.

"Andrés?" Vivo asked. He touched Andrés's hand gently, and then recoiled quickly. Andrés's hand was very cold.

Suddenly, Vivo realized that Andrés had passed away in his sleep. Vivo didn't know what to do.

Just then, Andrés's hand dropped Marta's song, sending it flying into the air coming in from the balcony windows.

"Oh no!" Vivo shouted.

But it was too late. A gust of wind picked up the song written on the piece of paper, sending it out the window!

Vivo leaped into action, chasing the piece of paper as it soared in the sky. He

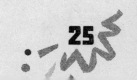

jumped from each rooftop until it made its way down the street. Vivo ran down to the sidewalk, never taking his eyes off the piece of paper. At every corner, someone threatened to get in his way—tourists snapping photographs of palm trees, shop owners calling out their daily specials, locals preparing fish on counters—but somehow, Vivo managed to dodge them all.

Finally, just when Vivo was starting to lose energy, he caught up to the flying paper! It landed on the plaza floor, just steps away from Vivo and Andrés's performance spot.

Vivo clutched the song and held it close

to him. He could not believe he would never see his friend Andrés again. What was Vivo going to do without his best friend?

"Adiós, *my friend*," Vivo said sadly, looking up toward the sky.

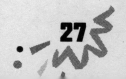

Chapter Five
The Vigil

The next few days were difficult for Vivo. He spent most of that time playing Andrés's favorite songs and instruments, in honor of him.

Soon after, a vigil was held in honor of Andrés. Vivo saw the usual group of friends Andrés had, but also a lot of new faces. They all gathered around the

Plaza Vieja. Some people hugged as others wiped tears away.

Montoya was standing in front of a palm tree, holding a piece of paper. As more people started to gather around, Montoya cleared his throat, ready to speak.

Vivo clambered up a tree to listen.

"Havana lost a good friend in Andrés Hernandez. His music filled our city and our hearts," Montoya said. "Señora? Would you like to say a few words?" Montoya gestured to a woman with shiny black hair in a long black dress. She nodded and walked forward in front of the crowd.

"Gracias," the woman said, thanking him. "I am Rosa Hernandez. Andrés was my late husband's uncle. My daughter Gabriela and I came all the way from Florida to be here today, to honor him. He meant a lot to my husband, and to our family. I am sad this is our first trip to Cuba."

Rosa patted her eyes as tears started to gather. Vivo felt emotional, too.

"Psst!" a girl whispered up to Vivo. She was short in stature, with wild purple hair and stacks of bracelets covering her arms. She wore large, bright pink glasses, and all her clothes were very mismatched.

Vivo looked over at her incredulously, shocked anyone would try to interrupt this moment.

"That's my mom," the girl continued. "My name is Gabi. And you're Vivo, right?"

Vivo nodded, and then quickly turned his head back to Rosa, hoping Gabi would get the hint that he was trying to listen.

"My husband's connection to Cuba was never broken," Rosa continued. "In fact, Tío Andrés inspired my husband to play music. And to teach music to our daughter. I guess you could say they had an unbreakable bond."

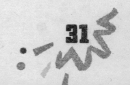

"Unbreakable *bonds*," Gabi said to Vivo. "That's what we got. We're family, right?"

Vivo looked at Gabi, slanting his eyes.

Gabi saw him looking back at her and took that to mean he was on the same page.

"See?! You get it! I have an idea. . . . Why don't you come live with me in Florida?!" Gabi suggested loudly.

Vivo continued gaping at Gabi, who clearly was unaware that other people were starting to notice her talking.

"Look, I have my backpack with me! Just hop in and you can come home with us tomorrow. Come on!" Gabi pointed at her colorful backpack. She reached over

to help him in, prompting Vivo to chirp angrily at her and run into the shadows of the plaza, where he could hide.

"Wait! Vivo! Where are you going?" Gabi whispered loudly.

Finally, Rosa looked over at Gabi and shook her head. Gabi's cheeks flushed and she stayed quiet, but still studied the plaza, searching for Vivo.

"Gabriela and I want to thank all of you for receiving us with open arms. *Gracias*," Rosa finished.

Then Rosa walked toward a picture of Andrés and laid a flower by it, before going over to Gabi and hugging her closely.

One by one, the mourners started to gather around the picture frame, leaving their own flowers or memories of Andrés by its side. Montoya played one of Andrés's songs, and people listened, crying and hugging each other.

It was almost dark before Vivo saw the last of the group turn away, leaving behind flickering candlelight.

Vivo walked over to Andrés's picture and sat in front of it. He looked around, teary-eyed, still not believing that his best friend was gone. And though it hurt Vivo to do it, he decided to sing one more song in honor of his friend and musical partner.

This is for you, Andrés, Vivo thought.

Vivo sang and sang, until his heart felt like it would burst. Soon enough, light started descending onto the plaza. The night had turned into morning. Vivo watched as people walked around the plaza, starting their mornings like it was a perfectly normal day, even though Vivo felt far from normal.

Just then, Marta's song fell out! Vivo picked it up quickly, not wanting to nearly lose it a second time. Suddenly, he had an idea. He felt determined for the first time in a long time. He knew what he had to do.

Chapter Six
The Idea

Vivo was sitting on the Malecón wall, watching Gabi nearby, who was attempting to play the harmonica. Rosa was packing up their suitcases, making sure everything was in order before she and Gabi returned to Florida.

Vivo decided to get a closer look, but stayed out of sight. There was no way he

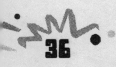

was going to let Gabi talk to him again. Or try to put him into her tiny backpack!

"Gabi, what are you doing?" Rosa asked.

"I'm playing a tune for Vivo, Mom. Maybe he'll hear it and decide to come to Florida with us!" Gabi said.

Gabi kept playing the harmonica. Vivo cringed. To him, it just sounded like noise!

"Gabriela, what did I say? No more pets!" her mom exclaimed.

Gabi dropped down to her knees and clasped her hands together, begging.

"NO," Rosa said firmly. "Besides, we cannot take a wild animal on a plane.

They will never let us back into the United States with him."

"Pleeeeease," Gabi said, wailing. "I promise—" Gabi started to continue, but was interrupted by Montoya, who was running up the street clutching a large case.

"Señora Hernandez! I am so glad I caught up with you before you left," he said. Montoya placed the case down in front of them. It was Andrés's drum case!

Vivo shifted nervously. He didn't know how he felt about Andrés's case being given to someone.

"Gabi, *mi Niña*, I know you love music, just like your uncle Andrés. Would you

like to keep one of his musical instruments?" Montoya asked.

Gabi's eyes widened and she nodded enthusiastically.

Montoya smiled. He opened the case to reveal maracas, accordions, and other small instruments.

"Whoa!" Gabi shrieked.

Vivo looked into the case. Just then, he noticed a small space in the back of it.

I could fit in there, he thought. He realized this might be his only chance. He started sneaking closer and closer to Gabi and the drum case.

Gabi picked up the accordion. She struggled to play it.

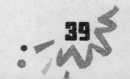

Rosa chuckled nervously.

"Thank you, Montoya. You gave my wild child an accordion," she said.

Montoya shrugged and gently put his hand on Gabi's back. "Music is in her blood."

"I love Cuban music!" Gabi shouted.

Vivo covered his ears, and then saw them all turn away to watch some pedestrians arguing in the street. He hopped into the drum case and hid under some instruments.

"Marta, here I come," Vivo whispered.

"Thank you, Gabi, for that beautiful song. I think all of Cuba knows you're here now," Rosa said sarcastically.

"Sorry, Mom. I know my playing can get a little too hardcore sometimes," Gabi said, grinning.

Inside the drum case, Vivo was horrified. *"Playing? That noise was playing?"* he asked himself.

Montoya laughed and he and Rosa said their goodbyes.

Gabi played another quick little tune and then tossed the accordion back into the drum case. Vivo gulped. There was no turning back now! Gabi zipped up the case just as a taxicab pulled up beside them. He felt the case get jostled around for a second until the car trunk closed. He was off to the Mambo Cabana!

Chapter Seven
Key West, Florida

It was a long trip to Florida. *"Where am I...? What time is it?"* Vivo said to himself groggily.

He looked around the drum case and noticed a small hole where the zipper was. He shifted toward the hole and peeped out of it.

Outside, he could see a large and

colorful kitchen. There were flowers in vases and sunlight pouring in from a large window over the sink. Beside it lay a small microwave which read 10:03 a.m.

Vivo sighed in relief.

"I still have eleven hours to get to the Mambo Cabana in time," Vivo said.

Suddenly, he heard something coming from outside the drum case.

"Look what I got! Are you excited about today?" Rosa asked Gabi.

"Of course! What's today . . . ?" Gabi wondered.

"It's your first cookie sale with the Sand Dollar troop!" Rosa exclaimed.

Rosa started unwrapping some frozen

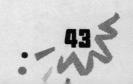

empanadas and placed them on a plate, while Gabi rolled her eyes.

"Yeah ... about that. I don't think that's going to happen. I've taken the Sand Dollars about as far as I can," Gabi said. To avoid her mom's gaze, Gabi took the plate of empanadas and popped them in the microwave, setting a timer for five minutes.

As the sound started on the microwave, Vivo took the opportunity to get closer to the zipper on the drum case, but he couldn't reach it without making noise. He decided to try to reach with his tail. Success! He looped his tail onto the zipper.

"You just started with the Sand Dollars," Rosa said. "It takes time to get to know them."

Vivo tried to pull the zipper down, but it got caught in his tail. *"Aaaayyyy!"* he squealed under his breath.

"Please give them a chance, Gabriela," Rosa continued. She sat at the counter and gave Gabi a stern look.

"Look, Mom, it's too late. I've already made my resignation video," Gabi said, showing her mom her phone. Gabi started to play a clip for her mom, wherein a video of Gabi popped up against a picture of the Sand Dollars and said, "See ya!"

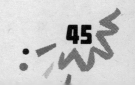

Rosa couldn't help but laugh at Gabi's creativity. Then she cleared her throat and turned serious again.

"Gabriela Maria Rosa Hernandez! You are part of that troop. You made a commitment. They are counting on you and you can't just abandon them now!" Rosa said.

"Why not?" Gabi asked.

"*You* can't keep pushing everyone away. You have to try to get along with other kids. Otherwise, you'll just end up lonely," Rosa told her daughter.

Gabi shrugged her shoulders and pulled the empanadas out of the microwave.

Meanwhile, Vivo was still tugging at his tail, trying to get it free from the zipper.

Rosa walked over to Gabi and grabbed her lightly by the shoulders.

"Gabriela, listen. You're doing this. I let you dye your hair purple! You *so* owe me! You're going to the cookie sale today. You're going to take selfies and have fun and BOND with other girls. Now get that cute uniform on!" Rosa exclaimed.

Gabi opened her mouth to protest, but her mom stuffed an empanada in her mouth. She was not taking no for an answer. While Gabi chewed on an

empanada, her mom handed her the uniform.

"Get it on, now," Rosa said, before leaving the kitchen.

As soon as she was out of sight, Gabi hid the uniform in the microwave. She sat at the counter and continued to eat.

Vivo tried to listen, but couldn't hear anything.

I think they're gone now. Coast is clear. This is my chance, he thought.

He pulled on his tail, a little harder than before. Suddenly, he was free!

But just then, he felt the case start to move with his weight. It rolled off the counter and onto the floor. Vivo tried

to escape. He started scratching at the case.

Gabi watched all this take place in confusion.

She spat out some of her food and said aloud, "Uhhhh what is happening?"

Vivo kept scratching the case, rolling himself in the only direction he could: forward. He had no idea if he was making his way out of the house and to the Mambo Cabana, but he had to try!

But little did Vivo know that he had rolled himself directly into Gabi's room.

Gabi followed, clearly stunned by the moving drum case.

"It's fine. . . . Everything is fine," Gabi said nervously. She snuck over to her closet while Vivo spun himself in a circle.

She pulled out a pair of goggles, a hockey stick, and her ultimate weapon: silly string. She was ready. Gabi walked over to the case and carefully started to unzip it.

Inside, Vivo gasped.

"Aaaaaahhhh!!!" Gabi screamed joyfully, seeing Vivo inside.

"*Aaaaaahhhh!!!*" Vivo screamed back.

"Vivo! You came after all! You're here with us!" Gabi shouted.

Vivo tried backing into the drum case,

but Gabi pulled him out and squeezed him tightly.

"You couldn't resist following me, could you?" Gabi asked.

Vivo was caught. He nodded yes.

"So, you snuck into my bag?" Gabi asked.

Vivo nodded again.

"Is it because you love me?!" Gabi shrieked.

Vivo's eyes widened and he shook his head.

But Gabi didn't seem to notice. "I'm so glad you're here, Vivo. We're going to be best friends forever!" Gabi said, hugging him even tighter.

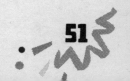

Vivo could not take that chance. He started struggling against Gabi, trying to get away.

"Forever's a long time, kid! I have a song to deliver! Nice meeting you, I'm out of here!" Vivo said.

Vivo ran toward the closest doors he could see, not realizing it was just Gabi's closet.

Suddenly, there was a knock on Gabi's bedroom door.

"Gabi? Is everything all right?" Rosa asked before starting to open the door.

"Quick! It's my mom. Hide!" Gabi whispered to Vivo.

Vivo just stared back at Gabi. There

was no way he was going to hide in her room. He had to try to get out through the door! Gabi, noticing his plan of action, nudged him gently with her hockey stick and pushed him into the closet, which was filled with piles of toys and clothes.

"What's up, Mom?" Gabi said, laughing nervously.

"Why was your Sand Dollars uniform in the microwave?" Rosa asked her, holding up the uniform.

"I was drying it," Gabi said matter-of-factly.

Rosa's eyes narrowed suspiciously. She walked into Gabi's room and

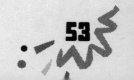

pointed at a bag of chips on the floor.

"What is THIS?" she asked, pointing to the bag.

Gabi quietly sighed with relief. Her mom hadn't noticed Vivo hiding in the closet!

"We can't have food in our rooms, Gabriela. How many times have I told you? It's going to attract animals!" Rosa said.

Gabi flashed a look toward her closet. If only her mom knew how close an animal *really* was. . . .

"Here," Rosa continued, handing Gabi the uniform. "Take your dry uniform and start getting ready for the cookie sale."

As soon as Rosa walked away, Gabi threw her uniform at the bed.

"See, Vivo? No one gets me, especially not my mom. She wants me to be like everyone else, but I'm not! I bounce to the beat of my OWN drum!" Gabi said.

Vivo climbed out of the closet and noticed the piece of paper with Marta's letter had fallen out of the drum case. Gabi noticed at the exact same time.

"No!" Vivo shouted, but it was too late.

Gabi grabbed the piece of paper and began to read.

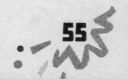

Chapter Eight
The Plan

As Gabi read the letter, Vivo decided to sneak out the window.

She was so engrossed with reading that she didn't even notice. Vivo grinned. He was free! He looked around at the bright sunshine and tall palm trees.

"*So . . . this is Florida, huh?*" Vivo said.

Gabi's neighborhood was very different from his neighborhood in Havana. Rows of houses lined the streets with bright green grass and flower gardens.

Vivo missed seeing the bustle of the Havana streets and the colorful houses and shops.

"Well, it's no Havana, but everyone's different, I guess," Vivo said.

He headed down the sidewalk, approaching the center of downtown Key West. To his right, he spotted a lawn full of pink plastic flamingos. Then a large group of tourists in Hawaiian shirts and cargo shorts started snapping pictures in front of the flamingos.

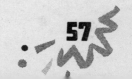

Vivo shrugged. *"Florida is weird,"* he said.

He turned away from the tourists before they could spot him. He had to find directions to Miami.

Suddenly, a bus pulled up behind Vivo with a billboard that read, MAMBO CABANA: ONE NIGHT ONLY.

An image of Marta graced the billboard. Vivo recognized her instantly. This was his chance!

People started to get off the bus while others lined up to get on. Someone asked the bus driver if the bus was heading to Miami and he confirmed it was.

Vivo was excited.

"Mambo Cabana, here I come!" Vivo cheered.

Vivo lined up behind the other passengers, trying to blend in. He pulled his cap down and adjusted the bandana on his collar.

But there was no way the other passengers wouldn't notice an animal trying to get on the bus!

"What is that thing?!" one passenger shrieked, pointing at Vivo.

"He has rabies!" another passenger yelled.

"Driver! Get him off the bus!" the passengers started to shout.

Plop! Vivo hit the ground and watched

the bus pull away. He barely had time to dust himself off before coming face-to-face with a scary-looking dog.

"Gulp."

Vivo took off running at full-speed, with the dog following closely behind.

Vivo tried remembering his way back to Gabi's neighborhood, passing the tourists now taking pictures in front of large palm trees and a sign that read, WELCOME TO KEY WEST! He hopped on a hedge and barely had a second to look around for a way out. That second was all he needed. In the distance, he saw a window wide open. He jumped and ran as quickly as possible, with the dog

barking and snapping his teeth.

In the nick of time, Vivo made it to the window and slammed it shut. The dog was barking hysterically outside and Vivo couldn't help but stick his tongue out at him.

"There you are!" Gabi suddenly yelled.

"Oh nooooo," Vivo moaned. He had unintentionally made his way back to Gabi's house!

"I know why you're in Florida," Gabi said. "You're here to deliver this to Marta."

Vivo had considered taking his chances and going back out into the street, but what Gabi said made him turn around and stare at her in surprise.

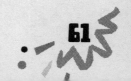

"I read Tío Andrés's letter from Marta. He wanted to be at the show tonight, didn't he? You came in his place," Gabi realized, sitting down with the letter in her hands.

Vivo nodded at Gabi.

"But why?" Gabi asked him.

Vivo took his hat off and pulled out the sheet music to Marta's song. He handed it over to Gabi, who read part of it. She looked from Vivo to the song, then the song to Vivo. She was smiling.

"Tío wrote Marta a song?" she asked.

Vivo chirped yes.

Gabi continued reading the song, and then she put it down.

As I prepare for retirement, I have been flooded with memories of the beautiful music we once made together. I don't know if you can forgive my silence since we were cruelly separated those years ago. Nothing would mean more to me than for us to sing together again.

My farewell concert is June 16th at the Mambo Cabana in Miami. If you are there with your tres, I'll know you feel the same. I hope is not too late.

Amor,

Marta

"But if you have this, that means Tío never got to tell Marta he loved her," Gabi said.

Vivo nodded again.

Gabi turned and looked at a photo of her father on her bedside table.

She took a deep breath and then stood up, looking determined.

"Vivo, this is important," Gabi said. "Marta needs to hear this song, so I'm going to help you get it to her."

Vivo gasped, completely surprised.

"We don't have much time, but don't worry, Vivo. I have a plan," Gabi said.

Vivo had never seen anything move more quickly than Gabi. She was like a

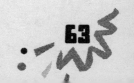

reckless tornado! One minute she was on her laptop looking up directions on how to get to Miami, and the next moment she was packing items into her backpack. Finally, Gabi turned to Vivo and motioned for him to get into the backpack.

Vivo knew this was his only option. He had to do this for Andrés.

Vivo hopped in and Gabi closed the backpack, leaving a small hole for Vivo to see and breathe out of.

"Mom?!" Gabi called. "I need to talk to you."

Vivo heard Rosa come into the kitchen.

"No. Whatever it is, the answer is no,"

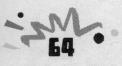

Rosa said. "I can see you don't have your uniform on."

"Mom, this is important. I need to go to Miami," Gabi said.

Rosa grunted, completely shocked by Gabi's request.

"It's Marta Sandoval's last show ever! Mom! It's not even that far!" Gabi pleaded.

"Since when are you a Marta Sandoval fan?" Rosa asked her daughter, crossing her arms in suspicion.

"Since FOREVER!" Gabi said.

"Fine, then name one song," Rosa said, amusement crossing her face.

"Uhhh... 'Des... pa... cito'?" Gabi tried.

"Go get your uniform on. You're going

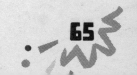

to that cookie sale. I'm not going to ask again," Rosa said.

Rosa walked away. Gabi slunk back to her room and threw the backpack on the bed. Vivo groaned.

"Sorry, Vivo," Gabi said, pulling him out of the backpack. Then she grabbed her laptop. She looked defeated for a split second, but as Vivo was starting to learn, nothing could stop Gabi.

"Don't worry, Vivo. Like I said, I have a plan. This is Plan B. If my mom won't take us, then we'll have to find our own way. Let's see. . . ," Gabi said, looking at the bus schedule for Key West.

"Perfect! This bus will get us there just

in time for the show!" Gabi said. Vivo hopped back into the backpack and he and Gabi snuck out of the house.

"Mambo Cabana, here we come!" Gabi said, strapping on her bike helmet. Then they were off!

Vivo was nervous but hopeful. Would their plan to get to Miami really work?

Chapter Nine
The Sand Dollars

"Welcome to downtown Key West!" Gabi said to Vivo. "I wish I could give you the full tour, but first, we need to get those bus tickets."

Gabi sped over to a nearby vending machine in the center of the plaza. She pulled her wallet out of her bag, winking at Vivo, and then bought the bus tickets

and tucked them into the front of her backpack.

"Okay, we're ready. Now remember, stay in my bag at all times," Gabi told Vivo.

"Cookies! Cookies!" a group of girls suddenly called out. There was a group of young girls sitting nearby on a park bench selling cookies.

"Oh no, it's the Sand Dollars," Gabi hissed.

Gabi shuffled over behind a group of people, trying to blend in.

"I can't believe they're here. They're usually on the other side of the plaza! We've got to get out of here before they spot me!" Gabi said to Vivo.

As Gabi tried to slink away, she overheard one of the girls, named Becky, talking to a customer.

"Did you know the Everglades are home to two thousand different species of plants and animals? And did you know—excuse me, sir? Is that a *plastic* bag you're using? You can buy one of our *cloth* bags instead," Becky said.

Becky was the leader of the Sand Dollars troop, and as such, she found herself telling others what to do all the time. She was also a fierce environmentalist, which wouldn't be a bad thing except that she never stopped talking about it.

The customer looked confused.

"I just want a cookie," he said.

Gabi sighed loudly, unable to contain her annoyance. She was unaware that the group of people she was standing behind had moved away.

"Hernandez!" Becky shouted. Gabi had been caught.

"Oh . . . hello girls," Gabi said.

"Where's your uniform?" a girl named Eva asked Gabi. Eva was soft-spoken and generally very sweet, but Becky sometimes rubbed off on her.

"I totally thought the cookie sale was yesterday," Gabi said.

"But you weren't here yesterday either," Becky responded.

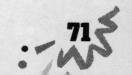

71

"Oh, good point. Well, I was busy," Gabi said.

The Sand Dollars looked unconvinced. They crossed their arms, waiting for another excuse. Gabi pulled Vivo out from her backpack and showed the girls.

"I was rescuing this animal!" she exclaimed.

Vivo groaned at Gabi, annoyed that he was being used for her excuse.

"Ooooh it's so cute!" Eva and Sarah, another girl, said.

"What's his name?" Eva asked.

"His name is Vivo. And he's an . . . opossum," Gabi said.

"That is NOT an opossum," Becky said.

"That's a kinkajou. It's a very rare South American tropical rain forest mammal! The honey bear."

The honey bear, Vivo thought to himself. *I like it.*

"Gabi, has he been to the veterinarian? He needs his vaccinations and at minimum, a week of observation," Becky said, eyeing Vivo suspiciously.

"A week?!" Gabi and Vivo both said.

"Well, he's already had all that," Gabi said, clearly lying.

"Then you'll have his vaccination records on him, won't you?" Becky said. "Hand them over." She stuck out her hand, waiting.

"Yeah, absolutely. They're in the trunk of my bike," Gabi said. "One sec."

She put Vivo back into her backpack and started to walk toward her bike.

"Plan B, Vivo," Gabi whispered to him.

"Wait, bikes don't have trunks, do they?" Eva asked.

"Girls, this Sand Dollar has gone rogue! Move out!" Becky shouted.

Gabi saw the girls scramble to get the cookies packed and run over to their scooters. She jumped on her bike and strapped on her helmet, just as the Sand Dollars reached their own scooters. Vivo hopped out of the backpack and into the basket on Gabi's bike.

Gabi started pedaling as fast as she could.

"We're going to have to catch the bus at the next stop, Vivo!" Gabi shouted.

The Sand Dollars were on electric scooters, gaining on Vivo and Gabi quickly.

"Pull over, Hernandez!" Becky shouted.

"Not a chance!" Gabi shouted back.

"Surrender the kinkajou!" Becky said.

"Don't worry, I'll lose them!" Gabi told Vivo. Then she started pedaling in another direction.

"The bus! What about the bus?!" Vivo chirped. But he knew Gabi couldn't understand.

"Lose them!" Gabi shouted at Vivo.

The scooters seemed to move faster, but Gabi had the bus in sight. It started going over the bridge.

"Oh no," Gabi said.

As soon as the bus crossed the bridge, the drawbridge began to rise.

"We're going to jump. Hold on tight, Vivo!" Gabi said. "Miami, here we come!"

Gabi pedaled hard and made it onto the bridge, but she was too late. Her only option was to go back, or to jump into the sand barge passing by underneath.

"*Oh no!*" Vivo cried.

Gabi made sure her helmet was strapped tightly, then made the jump.

They landed safely in some sand containers and escaped the Sand Dollars.

From above, the Sand Dollars looked down at the sand barge floating away.

"Eva, we're going to need your dad's boat," Becky said, watching Gabi and Vivo leave Key West.

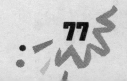

Chapter Ten
The Sand Barge

Gabi and Vivo slowly climbed out of the piles of sand they landed on.

"The song! Where is it?" Vivo cried.

He started digging around the sand frantically until he found it and put it back under the safety of his hat.

"Okay, now where's that bus? OH NO!" Vivo cried again.

78

He looked around him to see mountains of crates and sand, and beyond that, water. From afar, he saw the bus driving by on another bridge, in a completely different direction.

"Wheeeee!" Gabi shouted.

Gabi was rolling around in the sand happily.

"Vivo, you should really try this," she said. She was making sand angels.

Vivo looked at her in confusion. How could she be having so much fun when they missed their bus to Miami?

"Don't worry so much, Vivo. I've got a another plan. We'll take a shortcut through Everglades National Park and

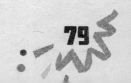

then we'll make it to Miami. No worries!" Gabi said.

Vivo didn't feel convinced. He started trying to make his own plan to get out of there and to the Mambo Cabana. Next to his sand pile, he spotted a deflated life raft and began heading toward it.

Once he reached it, he blew it up and threw it into the water, where it floated perfectly.

"Vivo! Great idea!" Gabi shouted. She threw her bike toward the life raft before Vivo could stop her.

Pop!

"Ah man, I thought the life raft could

hold it," Gabi said as Vivo watched the life raft deflate.

Vivo was upset. *"That was our only chance to get to Miami! You don't have any real plans! Your 'plans' are just bad impulses. And now we're stuck on this boat!"* Vivo shouted.

While Vivo shouted, Gabi started making her own raft.

"Ta-da!" she said when she was done.

Vivo blinked a few times, completely surprised.

"That will never float," Vivo chirped.

Gabi pushed the raft into the water, and it floated perfectly.

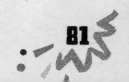

"Never thought that would work," Vivo said.

"Let's go, Vivo!" Gabi said, and before he knew it, Vivo was thrown onto the raft. He screamed, but landed on the raft safely. Then he started chirping angrily at Gabi again. She was really out of control!

"Heads up!" Gabi shouted, then jumped off the barge.

She missed the raft and landed in the water. Vivo panicked for a small moment, but soon enough, Gabi came out of the water laughing hysterically while pulling herself onto the raft.

Unable to resist, Vivo smiled at Gabi,

who was still laughing uncontrollably.

"Marta, here we come!" Gabi said, directing the raft toward the Everglades.

Meanwhile, in Key West, Rosa noticed Gabi hadn't come home from the cookie sale yet. She dialed Gabi's cell phone several times, with no luck.

"Gabi, I keep texting you," Rosa said into Gabi's voicemail. "Please call me back."

Rosa walked into Gabi's room and looked around. Then she saw Gabi's computer still open. The home screen showed the website for the Mambo Cabana.

"No . . . she wouldn't dare," Rosa said.

Then she clicked another tab, revealing the bus schedule to Miami.

"Guess she *would* dare," Rosa said.

Rosa sighed loudly and left Gabi's room in a hurry. She grabbed her car keys and pulled out of her driveway.

"Mambo Cabana, here I come," she announced.

Chapter Eleven
Everglades National Park

Vivo and Gabi had been floating on the raft for what seemed like forever. But somehow, Gabi seemed to know where to navigate the boat. They were finally entering Everglades National Park! Vivo pulled out Marta's song and read it for a moment before putting it back under his hat.

Taking a momentary break, Gabi watched Vivo and asked, "Vivo, are you scared?"

Vivo looked up at her.

"You know, my dad used to sing to me when I was scared. I can sing to you, if you want. . . . We could even sing Marta's song!" Gabi offered.

Before Vivo could protest, Gabi started beatboxing. Vivo winced. She was terrible at it! Then Gabi started tapping on her body with her hands, like a drum.

"Drumming's in my blood. I can teach you!" Gabi said.

Vivo couldn't help himself as he laughed out loud.

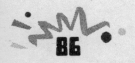

"You're going to teach me how to play the drums," he said incredulously.

Gabi reached over the edge of the water and pulled off some branches from nearby trees to use as makeshift drumsticks.

"Here, hold your drumsticks like this. Now try this simple beat," Gabi said, demonstrating.

"That's just noise," Vivo said to himself.

Vivo repeated her beat, then did another simple beat against the raft.

"Wow, you're a quick learner!" Gabi said. "I'm such a good teacher!"

Vivo rolled his eyes.

Then the two of them started drumming

beats together. Before long, they were both getting really into it. Gabi laughed and Vivo couldn't help but smile. He couldn't believe they were creating a rhythm together. Maybe she wasn't so bad after all. . . .

Suddenly, they heard a large thunderclap overhead. The sky started to darken and it began to rain lightly.

Vivo hopped over to the sail and held on to it tightly. He was scared.

"Don't worry, Vivo. It'll probably blow over soon. It's just a little bit of rain," Gabi said. But she looked scared too.

Before long, the wind started picking up, and the raft started moving violently

against the water. It started to rain so hard that they could barely see each other on the raft.

Then the raft started to spin and crashed into some tree roots at the bank of the swamp. The howling wind pushed Vivo's hat off his head. The song flew out of Vivo's hat.

"No!" Vivo cried.

"I'll get it, Vivo!" Gabi shouted, reaching for the song. At the same time, Vivo reached up, catching his hat, but when the raft started to spin again, he grabbed on to a tree for support. Meanwhile, Gabi and the raft floated away.

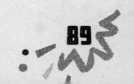

"Vivo!" Gabi cried. "Don't worry, I got the song!"

"Gabi!" Vivo shrieked.

And just like that, Gabi and the raft were gone, leaving Vivo all alone.

Vivo started to panic.

"The song's with Gabi. What am I going to do? I'm going to fail Andrés. I need a new plan!" Vivo shouted. "Gabi! Gabi!"

Vivo kept looking around wildly, but didn't see her anywhere. He looked up and spotted large birds.

"That's it! I need a bird's-eye view to find Gabi in this swamp. Hey!" Vivo shouted. "I need help!"

Vivo waved one of his arms wildly,

trying to hang on to the tree, but the wind was too strong. He fell from the tree and landed softly in a giant pile of dirt.

Vivo dusted himself off. Inside the swamp, the storm felt calmer, but Vivo didn't like seeing the dark surroundings. He looked around and saw some of the birds were perched on some nearby trees, waiting out the storm. Vivo approached one of the birds, who was on the ground digging a hole.

"Excuse me, I'm Vivo. I was separated from my friend. Maybe you could fly me up and help me find her?" Vivo asked.

"I'm Dancarino. Normally, I'd help a guy out, but I'm indisposed at the

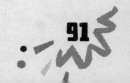

moment," the bird said. Dancarino continued digging.

"Why are you digging?" Vivo asked.

"I'm just going to take a long dirt nap," Dancarino responded. *"I'm hibernating until dating season is over."*

"Dating season?" Vivo asked curiously.

"All my life I've been told that I would find the girl of my dreams during the dating season. But I've been here for eight straight seasons and nothing. It's like I'm invisible! No one cares, especially not Valentina," Dancarino said, motioning to another bird standing alone on a tree.

Suddenly Valentina looked over at Dancarino.

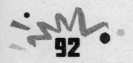

"Oh, she's looking at me! Good luck finding your friend! Bye, Vivo!" Dancarino said, using his wings to scoop dirt all over himself and bury himself in the hole.

Vivo pulled Dan's head out of the dirt.

"Wait! Have you tried telling her how you feel?" Vivo asked.

"I can't tell her. . . . I'm scared she'll reject me," Dancarino responded. He dropped his head down low.

"I'm not letting another friend go through life without sharing his feelings. Come on, I'll help you and then you help me find my friend. Deal?" Vivo asked, putting his hand out for Dancarino to shake.

Dancarino raised his eyebrows at Vivo, but agreed to the deal.

Vivo grabbed Dan and led him to a spot underneath Valentina's tree branch.

"Introduce yourself," Vivo said, nudging Dan.

"Hi! You're Dancarino! I mean, I'm Dancarino!" the bird said, blushing.

"How enchanting," Valentina responded.

"Oh man, back to my hole," Dancarino said. He was getting nervous.

"No, you can do this," Vivo said encouragingly. *"Smile and compliment her."*

Dancarino took a big gulp and then said, *"Valentina, your eyes are like two huge pools . . . no, bayous on your face."*

"*Bayous on my face?*" Valentina asked, confused.

Vivo shook his head.

This is not going well, he thought to himself.

"That's the nicest thing anyone's ever said about my ey—AHH!!" Valentina said before falling into the water.

Valentina coughed and then continued. Vivo stared at her.

"*Um ... that's the nicest thing anyone's ever said about my eyes.*"

Never mind, Vivo thought. These two are perfect for each other.

"*Dancarino, you have such nice feathers,*" Valentina said.

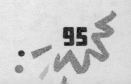

Dancarino giggled shyly.

"Now take her hand," Vivo whispered to Dan.

Dancarino reached out to grab Valentina's wing, but poked her in the face accidentally. Then Valentina tried, and poked Dancarino in the face.

"Sorry," they both said together.

Finally, the two of them held wings. Then they smiled and flew off together.

"Perfect!" Vivo cheered.

He was happy for his new friend. Then, Vivo realized they were gone and he was all alone again.

"Wait! You were supposed to help me! We had a deal!" Vivo shouted, but

Dancarino and Valentina were gone.

Vivo jumped into the tree vines and tried to swing toward the birds, but he got caught on a branch and fell into a bog.

"I'll be lucky to make it out of here alive," Vivo said, defeated.

Chapter Twelve
The Sand Dollars Arrive

Meanwhile, the storm had finally settled. Gabi looked around her to see a lot of wreckage from the storm. The raft was barely floating now and Gabi was covered in mud. But the worst part was that Gabi was separated from Vivo.

Suddenly, she realized something else was missing, too. "Oh no! Where is it?

Where's the song?" Gabi asked, looking around frantically.

Just then, Gabi spotted something in the distance. It was headed straight toward her. Gabi turned to the sail again, willing her destroyed raft to go in a different direction.

"Hernandez!" Gabi heard.

"Oh no," Gabi said to herself. "Becky?!"

"Where's the kinkajou?!" Becky asked, pulling up alongside Gabi's raft. The Sand Dollars were in a large boat, looking dry and perfectly in control.

"Um, yeah . . . about that. He's kind of missing right now," Gabi said.

"You lost a kinkajou in the Everglades?

Congratulations, Hernandez, you've killed him!" Becky said.

"Wait, what?" Gabi asked, startled.

"A kinkajou cannot survive in this environment. Every single animal here is his natural predator. You are going to help us find him," Becky said.

"I'm not helping you with anything," Gabi said.

"Then I guess I can recycle this," Becky said, holding up Marta's song.

Gabi gasped and pointed to the song.

"Where did you get that?" she asked.

"Doesn't matter. It's ours now. Eva, feel free to eat it now," Becky said, handing it to Eva.

Eva opened her mouth and was about to eat it, when Gabi finally gave in.

"Wait! Fine, you win. I'll wear the uniform. I'll sell the cookies. I'll do whatever you want, just give me the song back, please," Gabi pleaded.

"You'll get the song back when the kinkajou is with us," Becky said.

Gabi rolled her eyes, but knew this was her only option. She grabbed her backpack and jumped onto the Sand Dollars' boat, looking at the raft drift off into the distance.

Chapter Thirteen
Lutador

Vivo climbed his way out of the bog. He was in a full-blown panic now.

"Gabi!" he called. *"Where are you?!"* He continued climbing his way out, getting mud all over the place. Then he tripped on a branch and fell back into the mud.

"Ugh. Who am I kidding? I'll never get

out of here. Gabi!!" he shouted. But he knew she couldn't hear him. He continued calling for her anyway, knowing it was his only hope at getting to Miami.

"Shhhh," Vivo suddenly heard. Vivo turned around and saw an iguana shushing him. *"Be quiet,"* the iguana said.

"Seriously? You have no idea what I've been through these past few days. First of all—" Vivo started to say, but the iguana interrupted him by asking him to be quiet again.

"That's it! You want me to be QUIET? I AM BEING QUIET!" Vivo shouted. He had had enough.

The iguana's eyes widened and he ran away in fear.

"YEAH!" Vivo shouted after him, "THAT'S WHAT I THOUGHT. WALK AWAY IN THE MIDDLE OF A SWAMP! DON'T MIND ME."

Vivo started to wipe the mud off himself and walk away from the bog, when just then, he saw two very large, yellow eyes staring at him.

"Mmmm... what a lovely voice you have. I've never seen you around these parts. My name is Lutador. What's your name?" Lutador the python asked, coiling his slithering body around a branch.

Vivo gulped. He had never seen a

snake in real life before. Lutador looked scary!

"*I'm . . . Vivo,*" Vivo said quietly.

"*I don't like that name. I'm going to call you Noisy. Because that's what you are. A noisy, singing rat,*" Lutador said, laughing.

"*I'm not a rat,*" Vivo said, shifting his feet nervously.

"*What are you then?*" Lutador asked, slithering closer to Vivo.

"*I'm a . . . kinkajou,*" Vivo responded, taking one step back.

"*Sounds. . . exotic. Well, listen here, my noisy kinkajou friend. There's one thing you should know around here. And that's*

that I hate noise. You want to live? Then stay quiet," Lutador said.

Vivo dared to look around and noticed a group of animals in various areas of the bog. He hadn't noticed them before because they were so silent.

"I'm sorry. I promise you won't hear a peep from me. I can do quiet!" Vivo said.

"Oh, I know you're going to be quiet. All my meals stay silent," Lutador said. Then he lunged toward Vivo! Vivo scrambled up a tree just in time, but Lutador was close behind him.

Vivo leaped and jumped from branch to branch. Just ahead, Vivo spotted a clearing. He was about to run out of trees

to jump on. Vivo turned around nervously and saw Lutador snap his jaws, narrowly missing Vivo's tail. Just as Vivo hurried closer to the clearing in the trees and thought all hope was lost, he felt himself get swooped away off the branches. For a moment, he thought he was dead. But then Vivo turned around and saw Lutador hissing from below in the trees.

It was Dancarino who swooped Vivo to safety!

Vivo hugged Dancarino tightly.

"I'm saved! Thank goodness," Vivo cried.

"I saved you, because love saved me," Dancarino said.

Just then, Valentina flew next to Dancarino. The two birds looked at each other lovingly.

"Don't worry, Vivo. We've got your back, amigo," Dancarino said.

"Don't worry your little ferret head," Valentina echoed. *"We will help you find your friend now."*

Vivo felt relieved. He took a moment to admire the view, and then the three of them flew off against the sky, searching below for Gabi.

Chapter Fourteen
Lutador Attacks

Gabi and the Sand Dollars had been floating by the embankment for a long time. They had called for Vivo, with no luck. Gabi knew they'd have to go deeper into the swamp to find him. And that meant getting off the boat.

Eva steered the boat and parked it against some tree roots.

"I think this is right around where I lost him," Gabi said. "Vivo!" she shouted. "Come on, Vivo!"

"No kinkajou, no song," Becky said. "Yell louder."

Gabi started yelling louder and louder. Then they all started walking deeper into the swamp. The other Sand Dollars helped Gabi by shouting too. Just then, Gabi heard a rustle in the bushes.

"Vivo? Is that you?" Gabi asked. "Stay there! Don't move!" Gabi hoped she could get to Vivo before Becky.

She approached the bushes and suddenly saw Lutador slither out!

"Snake!!" Gabi screamed. She was

really scared. "Everyone to the boat!"

Gabi started running toward the Sand Dollars and then they all began to run at full-speed. They arrived at the boat, but Lutador cut them off. They darted in a different direction, abandoning the boat.

The girls hid quietly in a small grove of trees.

"I think we've lost him," Becky said, putting her hands on her knees.

But suddenly Lutador slithered into a circle, surrounding the four girls with his body.

"This is not good," Eva said.

"You guys, before I die, I just have to confess, I don't always recycle!" Becky said.

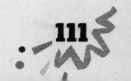

But no one seemed to hear her. The girls were all thinking of ways to escape.

"Here, guys, take this," Gabi said, handing them her backpack. They all pulled out random items and started throwing them at Lutador.

Gabi grabbed a container of her silly string and sprayed it at Lutador. He looked surprised, but unfazed. Then she threw the container at his face.

Lutador hissed at them.

"Get back!" Becky shouted, but Lutador started to close in.

The girls started screaming.

From up above, Dancarino, Valentina, and Vivo looked around. They could

hear the yells from down below.

"It has to be Gabi. She's in trouble. Let's go!" Vivo yelled.

Dancarino swooped down quickly.

"Hey, Lutador!" Vivo shouted, jumping off Dancarino to land on a branch above the snake.

Vivo snapped off two branches and began to drum on the tree trunk.

"Look who it is ... the noisy singing rat," Lutador said, taking his attention away from the girls.

"That's right. I'm noisier than ever!" Vivo said, drumming harder.

"Stop that noise!" Lutador shouted. *"You should know the rules by now."*

"*Come make me,*" Vivo said.

"*With pleasure,*" Lutador responded. He hissed and slithered over to Vivo.

"*Oh no,*" Vivo said. He hadn't quite thought his plan through. He just knew he had to protect Gabi and the others.

Lutador slid up toward Vivo and lunged at him, but Vivo jumped out of the way just in time. Vivo started swinging through the trees, remembering his days when he lived in the rain forest. It was like his body took over, knowing exactly what to do even though he didn't.

"You can do this, Vivo!" Gabi shouted from below.

"Gabi, a kinkajou can't beat a python!" Becky said matter-of-factly.

But Vivo did continue to jump away from Lutador's attacks, all the while singing and drumming against every tree.

Dancarino and Valentina dug a hole and jumped in to stay out of the way.

Vivo suddenly started to notice a pattern in the trees and the way Lutador moved. Just then, Vivo had a plan.

He dodged to the right and then to the left, creating a zigzag around the trees. Suddenly Lutador had tightly coiled himself around the trees. He was stuck!

"Enough is enough!" Lutador shouted. *"You can't run forever."*

115

"Watch me," Vivo said.

Vivo jumped down to the Sand Dollars and looked over at Lutador. The python couldn't move.

The Sand Dollars clapped for Vivo. He had saved them!

"Gabi!" Vivo chirped.

He jumped into her arms, hugging her.

"You totally took down that snake!" Gabi said proudly. "You are one crazy cool kinkajou."

All the girls circled around Gabi and Vivo and embraced.

Then they headed away from Lutador and back to the boat.

"So . . . can I have the song back?" Gabi

smiled widely and looked hopefully at Becky.

"Of course!" Becky said. Then she looked around and started digging through her pockets.

Vivo spotted the song on the ground and jumped out of Gabi's arms. He grabbed it, hoping it was saved, but it was too late. The song fell apart in pieces in Vivo's hands! Vivo was crushed.

The Sand Dollars and Vivo got on the boat and made their way back home to Key West. There was no point in going to Miami now. The song was gone.

Chapter Fifteen
One More Song

Marta Sandoval had just arrived at the Mambo Cabana. Outside, dozens of fans were already lined up, waiting to get into the venue for the show. They all clapped and cheered when Marta got out of her car and was ushered into the venue by the stage manager.

"We're so lucky that you're here,

Ms. Sandoval," the stage manager said.

Marta stopped to sign a few autographs. One of the fans had Marta sign an old photograph of her and Andrés.

"Is it true Andrés is coming to the show? Will he perform with you?" the fan asked.

"I hope so," Marta responded. She went inside and headed to her dressing room to get ready for the show.

Marta's dream to play at the Mambo Cabana had come true long ago, but she wished she could have shared that dream with Andrés. Inside her dressing room, she still had many pictures of him hanging up on the walls. Even though he

wasn't with her, he continued to inspire her music at every performance.

Marta was hopeful that he would make it to the show. She wanted to sing with him one last time.

Just then, she heard a knock at the door. "Come in," she called out.

The stage manager walked in, looking very upset.

Marta noticed that the stage manager was carrying a newspaper article.

It was Andrés's obituary.

"I'm so sorry, señora," the stage manager said, handing it to Marta before letting her have some time alone.

Meanwhile, Vivo, Gabi, and the Sand Dollars were gliding through the water on their way back to Key West. Vivo looked out over the water and spotted his reflection. He could barely recognize himself. He saw tears coming out of his eyes. He felt hopeless and defeated.

"So, what are you going to do now?" Dancarino asked Vivo, flying alongside the boat.

"I guess I'll go back to Cuba. Without the song, there's nothing for me here. I failed Andrés," Vivo said.

"No! Don't say that. You did everything you could," Dancarino said.

Vivo turned to look at him, wiping

away his tears. He had never felt so sad in his life.

"You don't understand. Andrés did everything for me. And when he needed me the most, I turned my back on him. This was my one chance, and I let him down," Vivo said.

Vivo started crying again and then he heard Gabi singing.

She was singing Marta's song!

Vivo quickly got to his feet and went over to Gabi. He snatched the recorder out of her backpack and started to play the melody while Gabi continued singing.

"Vivo! You know the melody!" Gabi

exclaimed. "And *I* know the lyrics!"

"We've still got the song!" Vivo chirped.

"The mission is back on!" Gabi said. "Turn this boat around! We're going to Miami!"

The Sand Dollars stared at Gabi in disbelief for a moment, but then they saw Vivo smiling up at them.

"You heard the kinkajou. Turn the boat around!" Becky demanded.

Eva made a wide turn and then started speeding off toward Miami.

Meanwhile, Gabi and Vivo started to try to perfect the song. Gabi still couldn't sing well, but she had remembered each lyric perfectly. Vivo slowly started to get

into the rhythm of the melody, jotting down the music notes on a piece of paper.

After a while, they had finished the song. They smiled happily at each other.

"It's done!" Gabi said. "Now we just have to find Marta and get this to her. Oh, and one last thing!"

Gabi grabbed the song from Vivo and wrote, BY ANDRÉS HERNANDEZ at the top, and, WITH HELP FROM GABI AND VIVO, at the bottom. Then she handed it back to Vivo, who put it in his hat for safekeeping.

"We make a pretty good team," Vivo said, smiling up at Gabi.

"Look, guys!" Eva shouted. "I can see Miami!" She pointed to the city in the distance.

Sure enough, the city lights of Miami started to come into view. They were dazzling! Vivo started getting tears in his eyes again, but this time from excitement.

"We're *never* going to make it in time!" Sarah said.

"We'll have to break a few rules then," Becky responded, taking over for Eva at the front of the boat. She headed for the city at full speed. Vivo held on to the deck railing, grinning from ear to ear.

 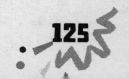

Chapter Sixteen
Miami

A short while later, the boat pulled up to the dock, and Vivo and Gabi jumped off. Becky handed them one of their electric scooters and a helmet.

"Good luck, you two," she said.

Vivo tipped his hat to her, then hopped into Gabi's backpack.

Gabi took off toward the city streets of

Miami. The twinkling lights reminded Vivo of Havana, and reminded him of all that he shared with Andrés. On nearly every light post, there was a poster of Marta, advertising her last show at the Mambo Cabana.

"We'll have to follow these signs and hope it gets us to the Mambo Cabana in time!" Gabi shouted.

Soon enough, the two of them pulled up at the Mambo Cabana. Flashing lights swept across the floor and the building, and now, what looked like hundreds of people lined up outside, cheering and waiting to get into the show. Gabi parked the scooter, and then she made

her way to the entrance. She snuck up to the front, right by the entrance doors.

"Tickets!" a ticket taker shouted at Gabi.

"Uh ... *no hablo ingles,*" Gabi said, pretending she didn't speak English.

"Yo tambien hablo español," the ticket taker responded, clearly unamused and speaking perfect Spanish right back to her.

Gabi looked around, trying to find a way into the building.

Suddenly, Gabi heard a sharp voice.

"Gabriela!" Gabi wheeled around to see her mom running toward her.

"Oh no! It's Mom!" Gabi exclaimed.

Gabi pushed past the ticket taker and ran inside the venue.

"Security!" the ticket taker shouted.

Men and women in black suits spotted Gabi and started running toward her. They were closing in. Gabi remembered the way Vivo dodged Lutador and started to do the same thing.

Just when Gabi thought she'd lost them, a security guard suddenly grabbed her.

"Gotcha!" he said.

"Let me go!" Gabi squealed, squirming to get out of his grasp.

Vivo jumped out of the backpack and roared at the security guard. On instinct, the security guard screamed at

the sight of him and dropped Gabi, who used the momentary distraction to slide through his legs and keep running. Vivo and Gabi made it into a corridor that was marked TALENT ONLY, but the door there was locked.

"What do we do?" Vivo asked.

Gabi looked around and noticed a window into a room. She pointed at it. Maybe it was Marta's dressing room!

"Vivo, hurry. Make it in and give the song to Marta. I'll hold them off," Gabi said.

Vivo chirped in protest, but Gabi was already shaking her head.

"Here," she said, pulling off one of her

bracelets. "This is a friendship brace-let. So you'll never forget me. Finish the mission, for the both of us."

Vivo looked into her eyes, touched by her gesture. Then he nodded and climbed toward the open window, just as security descended on Gabi, followed closely behind by her mother.

Chapter Seventeen
The Mambo Cabana

Vivo made it through the window. Gabi was right. It *was* Marta's dressing room.

As soon as he hopped down, he saw Marta sitting over the newspaper clipping, crying.

"Marta?" Vivo asked, but she didn't hear him.

He looked over to see a picture of Andrés

taped on her dressing room mirror. Vivo approached quietly and then gently touched Marta's arm, surprising her.

"Are you Vivo?" Marta asked, wiping away her tears. She had read about Vivo in Andrés's obituary.

Vivo nodded.

"You came all the way from Cuba . . . ? What are you doing here?" Marta asked.

Vivo took off his hat and pulled the piece of paper with the song out. With one last glance, he handed it over to Marta.

"*Para Marta . . . ,*" Marta read. "He wrote this for me?" she asked, placing her hand over her heart.

Vivo nodded again.

Marta began to cry as she read through the lyrics. Vivo was touched. He could see why Andrés had thought Marta was so special.

"Thank you. He never told me he felt this way," Marta said. Then she kissed the piece of paper. "I love you, too, Andrés."

Marta turned toward Vivo and gave him a hug, thanking him again and again.

For a brief moment, Vivo could feel Andrés there with him. He felt happy to be close to someone who had also loved Andrés.

Just then, there was a knock on the door.

"Señora!" the stage manager called. "We're ready for you."

Marta wiped away her tears and looked at herself in the mirror before nodding and getting up.

"I have to go," Marta said. "And now, thanks to you, I have a new song to sing."

Marta walked toward the door and turned to Vivo one last time.

"Andrés would be so proud of you, Vivo," she said. She blew Vivo a kiss and left him alone in her dressing room.

Vivo watched her go and smiled to himself. He had done it. He had helped his best friend, Andrés. His plan had

worked. Just then, a thought popped into his mind.

Gabi, he thought. He looked down at his arm and looked at the bracelet Gabi had given him. He touched it gently, and then ran out onto the balcony.

"Gabriela, I cannot believe you did this," Gabi's mother told her.

"Vivo needed to deliver a song to Marta!" Gabi responded.

"Do you hear yourself? This is crazy!" her mom said. She started to pull away from the Mambo Cabana parking lot.

"This is exactly why I didn't tell you. I knew you wouldn't get it. Only Dad

136

would," Gabi said, crossing her arms and looking at the lights outside. She didn't notice Vivo crawling out of Marta's balcony.

"Don't do this, Gabriela. He's not here. I'm here. And I know that's not the same. I know I'm not funny and I don't play music with you, but you can always talk to me about anything," her mom said.

Gabi turned around to face her mom. After everything she had been through to get to Miami, she suddenly felt brave and ready to talk to her mom.

"You don't even try to understand why this is important to me!" Gabi said. "Vivo understood."

"Vivo is in Cuba!" her mom responded.

Just then, Vivo landed on the windshield. Gabi's mom screamed, and then pulled the car over to the side of the road.

"Vivo!" Gabi yelled.

Gabi rolled down her window, letting Vivo climb into the car.

Then the two friends hugged.

"Did you get the song to Marta?" Gabi asked.

Vivo nodded.

"Yes! You did it!" Gabi said.

Vivo chirped at her.

"You're right. WE did it," Gabi said, correcting herself.

Rosa stared at the two of them, shocked.

"Wait, you were telling the truth?" Rosa asked.

Gabi and Vivo nodded.

"Well, that doesn't mean you can run off to Miami without telling me," her mom said.

Gabi sighed. "I know. I'm sorry, Mom. But I had to deliver Tío's song. He didn't get to tell Marta he loved her. Just like I never got to tell Dad how much I loved him before he died," Gabi said.

Suddenly, Gabi had started crying. Vivo held her hand, while her mother jumped out of the car and moved into the back seat with the two of them.

Then she hugged her daughter close.

"Your dad knew how much you loved him," her mother told her. "That kind of love lives forever."

Gabi was still crying, but she was smiling now.

Her mom smiled back at her, and then looked at Vivo.

"Welcome to the family, Vivo," Rosa said, embracing him in a hug. "All right. You two, buckle up. We've got a concert to get to."

Rosa hopped in the front seat and made a U-turn. They were headed back to the Mambo Cabana.

Rosa, Gabi, and Vivo made it back just in time. Marta was on stage and the crowd was applauding wildly.

"*Gracias*, everyone," Marta said into the microphone. "Thank you. To say farewell, I'd like to finish with one last song. It's a song written by an old friend, and delivered by new ones. . . ."

Marta looked over at them and winked. Then she started singing Andrés's song. It was more beautiful than Vivo could have imagined. Somehow, he and Gabi, and even Andrés, couldn't do it justice. Now Vivo knew exactly why Andrés had fallen in love with Marta. He was shocked that she had been able

to capture the song so perfectly after reading it one time. As Vivo listened, he imagined Andrés onstage with Marta. Andrés looked over at Vivo and smiled, and Vivo nodded at his friend one last time. He was so happy that he was able to fulfill his best friend's last wish. For Vivo, this was the best gift that he could have given him.

Table of Contents